Eeko's

Splash Landing

written by
Diane Charbonneau

illustrated by
Teghan Sargeant

 **FriesenPress**

Suite 300 - 990 Fort St
Victoria, BC, Canada, V8V 3K2
www.friesenpress.com

Copyright © 2015 by Diane Charbonneau
First Edition — 2015

ISBN
978-1-4602-6050-0 (Paperback)
978-1-4602-6051-7 (eBook)

1. *Juvenile Fiction, Science Fiction*

Distributed to the trade by The Ingram Book Company

Table of Contents

CHAPTER 1
Eeko Makes a Splash!............................ 1

CHAPTER 2
Mmm... Spaghetti!................................ 5

CHAPTER 3
What's Wrong With Orbat? 10

CHAPTER 4
Eeko Rides the Bus.............................. 14

CHAPTER 5
Eeko Goes To School............................ 17

CHAPTER 6
Eeko's Story... 21

CHAPTER 7
Fixing Orbat 26

CHAPTER 8
Oh No! No Fuel.................................... 32

CHAPTER 9
Eeko Goes Home.................................. 36

CHAPTER 10
Xavier Tells Eeko's Story 39

This book is for you Xavier
May God bless your little heart

CHAPTER 1

Eeko Makes a Splash!

Xavier gets off the school bus at his country home and runs to the backyard.

"Mom, I'm home," he shouts through the screened patio door.

Xavier hops on his four-wheeler and rearranges his baseball cap to shield his eyes from the late afternoon sun. He loves his ATV—the way the red paint shines in the sunlight and how much fun it is to ride.

Xavier turns the ignition key and smiles as the four-wheeler comes to life. As he gains speed, he zooms around the trees, through the sprinkler, around the above-ground swimming pool and around his brother's swing set.

Suddenly, a huge round object falls from the sky and splashes into Xavier's pool. The force of the object hitting the water is so great that it causes a huge wave of water to cascade over the edge of the pool. A few seconds later, the object bounces up into the air and lands unsteadily on the ground beside the pool.

What's that? It almost looks like a small spaceship, wonders Xavier as he steers his ATV towards the object. The glass dome is blurred by water drops, but he can see something moving inside just as the top hatch of the object moves. Xavier slams on the brakes and brings the four-wheeler to a stop. He gets off and very slowly approaches the object to investigate.

Wow! This really is a spaceship, he realizes in amazement.

All of a sudden, the hatch opens and Xavier comes face-to-face with an alien.

"Eeek!" they both scream.

Xavier runs one way around the pool to get away from the alien while the alien runs the other way around the pool. They bump into each other and scream, "Eeek!"

They dash around the pool in the other direction, just to bump into each other again. "Eeek!" they scream again.

They both stop, out of breath, and look at each other. Xavier notices that the alien has orange skin, shiny clothes and two strange-looking tentacles on the top of his head. At the end of each tentacle is an eye that rotates from front to back. *With four eyes, he must be able to see everywhere,* figures Xavier.

The alien sees Xavier's brown hair, two blue eyes and skin much paler than his own. They both have a nose, a mouth, two ears, two arms and two legs and are about the same size. They look very similar, but at the same time, strangely different.

"Hi, my name is Xavier. What's your name?" asks Xavier tentatively.

"I'm Eeko from planet Zeebot. I just crashed into your liquid container and damaged my spaceship, Orbat. It's in pretty bad shape; do you think you could help me fix it?" asks the alien as he points to his damaged space vessel.

"First of all, this is called a swimming pool, not a liquid container. It's for swimming and playing in the water," replies Xavier, chuckling. He examines Orbat's outer shell and adds, "I've never seen a spaceship before and I sure don't know how they work. But I'll try my best to help you."

CHAPTER 2

Mmm... Spaghetti!

"Xavier, supper's ready, time to come in," shouts Xavier's Mom from his house.

Eeko jumps back, frightened. His tentacles shoot straight up in the air, alerting him of possible danger.

"Who's that?" he asks.

"It's okay, that's my Mom. Want to come and eat supper with us?" asks Xavier. "I can ask my Mom if it's okay?"

"Um, okay, I'm really hungry. I've been in space for a long time," replies Eeko timidly.

"But first, we need to hide Orbat behind the shed so no one sees it," says Xavier.

Once the spaceship is well hidden beside the lawn-mower at the back of the yard, Xavier says, "Okay, let's go in—wait! We need to hide the two tentacles on top of your head. People don't have those on Earth and I don't want to freak out my Mom."

He removes his baseball cap and puts it backwards on top of Eeko's head.

"Perfect," says Xavier, "now you look a little more like me, except for your orange skin. If my Mom asks about the colour of your skin, you can tell her that you fell in some orange paint."

As they walk into the house, Xavier asks, "Mom, can my new friend Eeko stay for supper?"

"Of course he can, we're having spaghetti and meat-balls for dinner. But first, you both need to wash your hands," replies his Mom.

Xavier's Mom doesn't seem to notice anything unusual about his new friend, and neither does his Dad or younger brother, Max. *I guess they just accept my new friend even though he's a bit different,* Xavier thinks happily.

Things go smoothly until they sit down at the dinner table.

"Eeko, please remove your baseball cap, we don't wear hats during dinner," says Xavier's Dad.

Eeko panics and looks at Xavier for help, but Xavier just stares back at Eeko stunned. He's speechless.

"Please don't make me take off my hat," pleads Eeko in a panic. "That's really not a good idea. I don't think you want me to take off my hat."

Eeko looks at Xavier for help, but he gets nothing! Xavier's face has turned white as a ghost. *Oh no, think of something, say something!* Xavier tells himself.

"What is going on here boys?" asks Xavier's Dad as he looks from Xavier to Eeko. "The rule in this house is that hats are not allowed at the dinner table."

Finally Xavier finds his wits and quickly makes up an excuse. "Dad, Eeko's Mom cut his hair and did a terrible job. It looks ghastly and Eeko is very self-conscious about it. Could you make an exception just this one time, please? It won't happen again, I promise." Xavier knows he's telling a fib, but to avoid chaos, he has to keep Eeko's identity a secret.

Xavier's Dad ponders for a few minutes and says, "I see. I had a bad haircut when I was a kid too, so I think I know how you feel, Eeko. If taking off your hat makes you uncomfortable, you may keep it on." He examines Eeko for the first time and notices that Eeko's fingers are just a little too long for a kid his age and his ears are pointed and sit just a little too high on his head. He's also never seen orange skin before. He frowns and is just about to say something when...

"Oh thank you very much! It means a lot to me," says Eeko quickly.

"Wow! That was close, sorry about that, Eeko, I just panicked," Xavier whispers.

During dinner, Xavier's parents are deep in conversation and don't seem to notice that eating spaghetti is a challenge for Eeko. The long noodles are especially hard to eat and the meatballs sure make his cheeks round.

Xavier giggles and whispers to Eeko, "You're supposed to chew your food one bite at a time and then swallow it before you take another bite. Look how I do it." Xavier takes a bite of spaghetti and shows Eeko how it's done.

"On my planet Zeebot, the food is all liquids so you just drink it, but I'll give it a try," Eeko whispers back.

Once he gets the hang of chewing his food, Eeko really enjoys his spaghetti. *This is delicious. Maybe I could bring some back home with me when I leave,* wonders Eeko.

CHAPTER 3

What's Wrong
With Orbat?

After dinner, the boys run to the back of the shed to inspect the damage to Orbat. Eeko climbs in the cockpit to check out the instruments. He's very distressed. He knows it's going to be a challenge to find replacement parts for Orbat.

"Those two metal rods on top of the hatch are called transmitters. I need them to fly Orbat because they show the way back to Zeebot. They're not working; see how they're bent?" explains Eeko as he shows Xavier the metal rods.

"Right! New transmitters," says Xavier as he wonders how in the world he's going to find transmitters to fly a spaceship. *It's not like you can go to the hardware store and ask, 'Could I please buy two transmitters for a small spaceship?' I'd be the joke of the day,* imagines Xavier.

"I'll also need new landing gear," explains Eeko as he discovers that two of the three pads on the bottom of the landing gear have broken off.

"Of course, new landing pads," says Xavier sarcastically.

What in the world have I gotten myself into? What am I, a distributor for spaceship parts? Okay, okay, calm down. I need to get on board here and start thinking, ponders Xavier.

Xavier realizes that this is going to be a very challenging project and decides that he has to apply himself to the task at hand.

"All the scratches and cracks on Orbat's outer shell can be fixed with heavy-duty tape that my Dad keeps in the garage," says Xavier.

"Oh! I also need something to steer with," says Eeko. "When I accidently blasted off, I couldn't steer Orbat back to Zeebot. That's how I landed here on your planet."

"You couldn't steer your spaceship? That must have been scary! Don't worry Eeko, I'll do my best to find the parts we need to fix your spaceship."

It's getting dark outside now and Eeko is scared to spend the night inside Orbat all by himself on this strange planet.

"Earth is very different from Zeebot," explains Eeko, trembling from fear as dark shadows appear in the backyard. "There's no darkness on Zeebot, only daytime, probably because we have two suns."

"Two suns! Wow! You must really have to slop on the sunscreen. Maybe that's why your skin's so orange—too much sun," says Xavier.

Xavier sneaks Eeko into his bedroom for the night so that Eeko can feel safe.

"There, you can sleep here," says Xavier as he prepares a comfortable fluffy bed with blankets and pillows in his closet.

Both boys are so tired that they fall asleep right away.

CHAPTER 4

Eeko Rides the Bus

The next morning, Xavier has to go to school.

"It would be so much fun if I could go to school here on Earth. Would you take me with you, please?" asks Eeko.

Xavier shrugs and agrees. Besides, he can't let Eeko spend the day in his house with the babysitter and Max there. You never know what kind of trouble he could get into, especially if he makes noise and the babysitter comes to check it out. She'd call the police and then there would be a lot of explaining to do.

"You'll have to wear some of my clothes," says Xavier. "Your clothes are too different and shiny for regular clothes."

Xavier dresses Eeko in a pair of blue jeans, a printed Spiderman t-shirt and a clean pair of socks.

"It's great that we're both the same size," says Xavier, "your feet even fit in my old running shoes."

To finish off the look, Xavier puts his baseball cap on Eeko's head again.

"Just make sure you don't take off my baseball cap," advises Xavier. "Your tentacles are a sure sign that you're not from Earth. Just use the same story I told my Dad last night and everything should be okay. And don't forget that you fell in orange paint if somebody asks you about the colour of your skin."

"I won't forget," confirms Eeko.

As soon as Xavier's Mom and Dad leave for work, Eeko grabs a backpack in the closet and sneaks outside to join Xavier.

"Why is the bus taking so long to get here?" asks Eeko. "Too bad Orbat isn't working. It would be so much faster if we just flew to school."

"That probably wouldn't be a good idea; you'd start a panic. On Earth, people don't own spaceships—not yet, anyway. But it would sure be fun to fly around between trees and buildings," says Xavier as he runs around and between the trees with his arms spread out like the wings of a plane.

Finally, the school bus arrives and both boys climb aboard. Dave, the bus driver, takes a long look at Eeko.

"Is this a new student at your school, Xavier?" he asks.

"He sure is. This is Eeko, he comes from far away and he's coming to my school today," replies Xavier.

"Hello Eeko, nice to have you aboard. You can sit in the empty seat beside Xavier," says Dave as his gaze follows Eeko to the back of the bus. *Huh! Orange skin— probably a picky eater and only eats carrots,* he thinks to himself before continuing on his route to pick up other girls and boys.

CHAPTER 5

Eeko Goes To School

When the bus arrives at school, Xavier introduces Eeko to some of his friends.

"Eeko, this is Declan and James. They're in my class," Xavier says to Eeko. Turning to his friends, he says, "This is my new friend, Eeko. He's coming to class today."

"Hi Eeko, want to play on the structures with us?" asks Declan.

"It's a lot of fun, we race to see who can reach the top first," explains Xavier.

Eeko has never played this game before, but he's willing to try it with his new friends.

"Okay, when do we start?" asks Eeko.

"After 'READY, SET, GO', you start climbing," replies Xavier.

"READY, SET, GO!" shouts James. While the other boys run and start climbing up the structure, Eeko jumps high in the air and gets on top of the structure in one leap. The other boys are still climbing.

"Hey, how did you get here so fast?" asks Declan when he finally reaches the top.

"I guess I can climb the fastest," replies Eeko with a cunning smile.

Eeko realizes that he has special powers on Earth. He can jump higher than anyone else. He thinks to himself, *I wonder what other powers I have on this beautiful planet?*

Just then, the school bell rings. Eeko panics at the sound and tries to hide behind the play structure.

"Don't be scared. The bell just means that it's time to get to our class. Come with me," says Xavier as he heads for the entrance.

Mrs. Granda, Xavier's teacher, welcomes the students to class.

"Xavier, who's your friend?" she asks as Xavier and Eeko enter the classroom.

"This is Eeko, he's new here and this is his first day at this school," explains Xavier confidently.

"That's odd! The principal didn't advise me that we have a new student starting today. Not a problem, I'll get the information later. In the meantime, welcome Eeko. Why don't you sit in the row beside Xavier," says Mrs. Granda.

"Why is his skin so orange?" asks Olivia, one of the students.

Eeko timidly lowers his head and is just about ready to tell the orange paint story when Mrs. Granda explains, "Not everyone is the same, Olivia. We have to accept everyone's differences; that's what makes us all unique. Some people have white skin, others have black, red or orange skin like Eeko. We're all the same inside, and that's what counts."

Eeko likes Mrs. Granda. She makes him feel special and normal all at the same time.

During the day, Eeko finds all the subjects taught very interesting, but his favourite is geography. He's very happy to learn about the different continents and oceans on planet Earth.

CHAPTER 6

Eeko's Story

Every afternoon, Mrs. Granda invites a student to tell a
story. Today she asks Eeko.

Eeko is very happy to have been chosen. He gets up,
stands in the front of the class and begins.

"My story is about a little alien who went to school on planet Zeebot. In science class, each student had to build a spaceship as a special project. The teacher asked the students to press the ignition button on their spaceships to start the engines.

POP! POP! POP!

And the engines roared,

VROOM! VROOM!

The little alien pressed the ignition button on his spaceship,

POP! POP! POP!

and

VROOM! VROOM!

The engine on his spaceship started, but his arm accidently hit the take-off button."

All eyes are on Eeko, eagerly waiting for him to continue. "What happened next?" asks Declan.

"Well, the cover of the spaceship closed with the little alien inside and BLAST OFF!" shouts Eeko as he makes an upward motion with his arm. "The spaceship soared into the sky further and further away from Zeebot. The little alien's teacher shouted, 'Come back, come back!' But the little alien couldn't come back because he didn't know how to control his spaceship. The steering device had not yet been installed."

The entire class listens closely as Eeko continues. "The spaceship was spinning out of control as it passed by other planets. It was heading straight for a blue planet."

Eeko points to the globe of the Earth on Mrs. Granda's desk as he continues. "When approaching the planet, the little alien noticed that the blue was water just like on Zeebot, and there seemed to be ground where his spaceship could land."

Eeko takes a deep breath, clears his throat, and goes on. "The spaceship approached Earth and headed for what looked like a very small lake.

SPLASH!

The spaceship plunged into a swimming pool in someone's backyard and bounced right out for a safe but clumsy landing on the ground."

Before Eeko can continue his story, the bell rings to signal the end of classes for the day. The students want to stay to hear what happens next, but Mrs. Granda reminds them that their buses are waiting outside to take them home.

"Thank you, Eeko," says Mrs. Granda, smiling. "You're an amazing and convincing storyteller. It was so interesting that you may finish your story on Monday. Class, have a great weekend."

"We can't wait to see you on Monday to hear the end of your story, Eeko. Welcome to our class!" shout the students as they leave the classroom.

During the bus ride home, Xavier is worried about Eeko.

"Eeko, is that what really happened to you?" he asks.

"Yes," replies Eeko in a low voice. "I'm really worried that we may not be able to find the parts to fix Orbat and I won't be able to return to Zeebot."

CHAPTER 7

Fixing Orbat

When they arrive home, Xavier asks his Mom, "May Eeko stay for a sleep over? His Mom said it's okay. Please!"

Xavier knows that he's telling another fib, but he's sure that Eeko's Mom would have said yes so that Eeko doesn't have to sleep outside.

"As tomorrow is Saturday and there's no school, I think it would be okay," agrees Xavier's Mom.

The boys get to bed early, as they know tomorrow will be a very busy day fixing Orbat.

The next morning at breakfast, Xavier's Dad mentions that he needs to mow the lawn that afternoon. Xavier panics—the lawnmower is stored behind the shed where the spaceship is hidden.

"Dad, don't worry, I'll mow the lawn for you," says Xavier anxiously.

"Thanks Xavier, but I'll do it. The lawnmower's been acting up lately and I'd prefer to do it myself just in case there's a problem," replies his Dad.

Xavier and Eeko look at each other in alarm.

"We have to fix the spaceship quickly before my Dad gets the lawnmower," whispers Xavier. "That gives us very little time to get it done and have you blast off."

"Well let's get started then," says Eeko eagerly.

Xavier and Eeko quickly finish breakfast and run outside.

"There's a bunch of old stuff in the garage, let's go look there," says Xavier.

They find several boxes full of books, old toys, wires, tools and other stuff.

"What's this furry thing?" asks Eeko as he grabs something from one of the boxes.

"It's called a teddy bear. It's a stuffed toy that I used to cuddle at night, so I wouldn't feel alone."

"Oh! Do you think I could borrow it?"

"Sure, you can have it if you want, I don't need it anymore."

As they keep looking, Xavier finds something interesting.

"Hey, what about using this joystick from an old video game set to steer Orbat?" suggests Xavier.

"I think that could work. We'll have to try it out," agrees Eeko after examining it.

Xavier then finds a TV antenna that his Dad used a long time ago to watch television and shows it to Eeko.

"This object has two metal rods. I could easily find the signal to get back to Zeebot by attaching it on top of the hatch," says Eeko, nodding excitedly.

As the search continues, Xavier finds the tape to cover the scratches and cracks on Orbat's outer shell.

"I can't find anything in here that could work as landing gear," says Eeko. "I need two pads to attach to Orbat's legs or I won't be able to land."

Xavier thinks and thinks, then slowly his face lights up.

"I know what you can use for the landing gear," says Xavier excitedly, "the running shoes you have on your feet! We could attach them to the legs that are missing pads."

"Good idea, Xavier, they seem stable enough to cushion a landing," says Eeko as he checks out the bottoms of his shoes.

They pick up all the parts, run behind the shed and get to work repairing Orbat.

First, Xavier tapes the scratches and the cracks. Then Eeko removes the damaged transmitters from the hatch and with Xavier's help, reconnects the wires to the television antenna.

Next on the list, Xavier and Eeko install the joystick to the control panel. After a few adjustments, Eeko is confident it will work.

"Okay, one last part—the landing gear," says Xavier.

Eeko removes his running shoes. As Xavier tilts Orbat, Eeko ties Xavier's old running shoes to the legs.

"We're done! Hurray! Orbat is ready to fly back to Zeebot!" they shout happily, waving their arms up in the air.

"And just in the nick of time—my Dad will be coming back here soon to get the lawnmower," adds Xavier.

CHAPTER 8
Oh No! No Fuel

Eeko's excitement turns to a frown, and then tears as he realizes he forgot the most important thing of all: FUEL.

"Orbat is ready, but I need fuel to get back to Zeebot," says Eeko sobbing. "I don't think you have the kind of fuel I need for my spaceship."

Eeko folds his arms as he slowly crouches down to the ground with his head tilted forward. Even his tentacles with eyes are drooping down.

Without looking up, Eeko explains, "The fuel is very abundant on Zeebot, it's a small kernel that pops when heated. When you put a bunch of them in the tank and press the ignition button, the kernels heat up very quickly and start popping. When a bunch of them have popped, you press the take-off button and the spaceship blasts off into the sky."

Eeko slowly lifts his head and says to Xavier through teary eyes, "Now I'll never get back home to my family. My Mom and Dad must be wondering what happened to me. I've been gone a long time."

Xavier wasn't listening to Eeko—he was thinking about popping kernels.

"POPCORN! We could use popcorn! They're kernels of corn that pop when you heat them up!" shouts Xavier excitedly.

He runs into the house and comes rushing back a few minutes later with a jar full of popcorn kernels. Eeko's tentacles shoot straight up on his head, and his four eyes are staring at the jar of popcorn kernels.

"Where did you get that? These kernels look the same as the ones we use on Zeebot to fuel all our spaceships," says Eeko eagerly.

"Here, take them, I'm sure there's enough here to get you home," says Xavier.

"Thanks! Thanks a lot!" replies Eeko, smiling.

As they add the final touches to Orbat, Eeko senses a presence approaching. He stretches his tentacles around the shed and sees Xavier's Dad approaching. "Oh no! Your Dad's coming!" says Eeko as he dumps the whole jar of kernels in the tank.

Quick as a whip, Xavier pushes the lawnmower to the middle of the backyard.

"Here you go, Dad," says Xavier as he reaches his Dad.

"Thanks son, I'll take it from here," replies his Dad as he heads for the front yard.

"Phew! I just bought us a little time," says Xavier as he rushes back to Eeko.

CHAPTER 9

Eeko Goes Home

Eeko is happy and ready to go home to his family, but at the same time, he's sad to say goodbye to Xavier.

"You're a special friend, Xavier, and I'll miss you very much. Thanks for helping me fix Orbat—I couldn't have done it without you."

Xavier is very proud that he was able to help his new friend, but he's sad, too. "And I'll miss you. It was so much fun helping you. I hope I'll see you again someday."

Eeko opens his hands, palms up, and Xavier opens his hands, palms down, and they touch each other's hands. *It must be a Zeebot handshake,* figures Xavier.

"Once Orbat has all the right parts, I may just come back for some more of that spaghetti food stuff. I could even take you for a ride in outer space, if you like," says Eeko.

"Wow! That would be great," replies Xavier, smiling from ear to ear. "Goodbye for now, Eeko, and have a safe flight home!"

Eeko climbs into his repaired spaceship, holding the teddy bear Xavier gave him under his arm. He sits at the controls and presses the ignition button.

After a few sputters, you can hear popcorn popping then VROOM, the engine comes to life. Eeko waves one last farewell, and presses the take-off button.

BLAST OFF!

Orbat soars into the sky at lightning speed, and just as quickly disappears into the clouds.

Xavier slowly climbs on his four-wheeler and rides around the shed, the pool and the swing set while looking at the sky, wondering if he'll ever see Eeko again.

CHAPTER 10

Xavier Tells Eeko's Story

Monday is just another school day for Xavier until he gets to class. All his classmates want to know where Eeko is so that he can finish his story of the alien.

"Eeko has gone back to his old school, but he's told me the rest of the story and asked that I finish it for him!" says Xavier.

And so Xavier stands in the front of the class and tells the rest of the story about an alien from Zeebot, as it really happened.

When he finishes the story, the entire class stands and applauds loudly.

"Great story!" the students shout.

Xavier looks out the window up at the sky, and with a twinkle in his eyes, thinks of Eeko. *If only they knew that this is your story, Eeko—you're the alien from Zeebot! I know I'll see you again someday, my new friend!*